No One But You

NO ONE BUT YOU

Douglas Wood

ILLUSTRATED BY P.J. Lynch

CANDLEWICK PRESS

There are so many things in the world,

so many important things
to be taught,
to be shown.

But the best things,
the most important ones of all,
are the ones no one can teach you
or show you
or explain.

No one can discover them
but you.

No one but you can feel the rain kiss your skin
or the wind ruffle your hair.

And no one but you can walk through a rain puddle
in your bare feet.

No one but you can listen with your ears
to the song of a redbird in a treetop
or the wind in the pines
or the scolding of a squirrel as he
shakes his tail and stamps his feet.

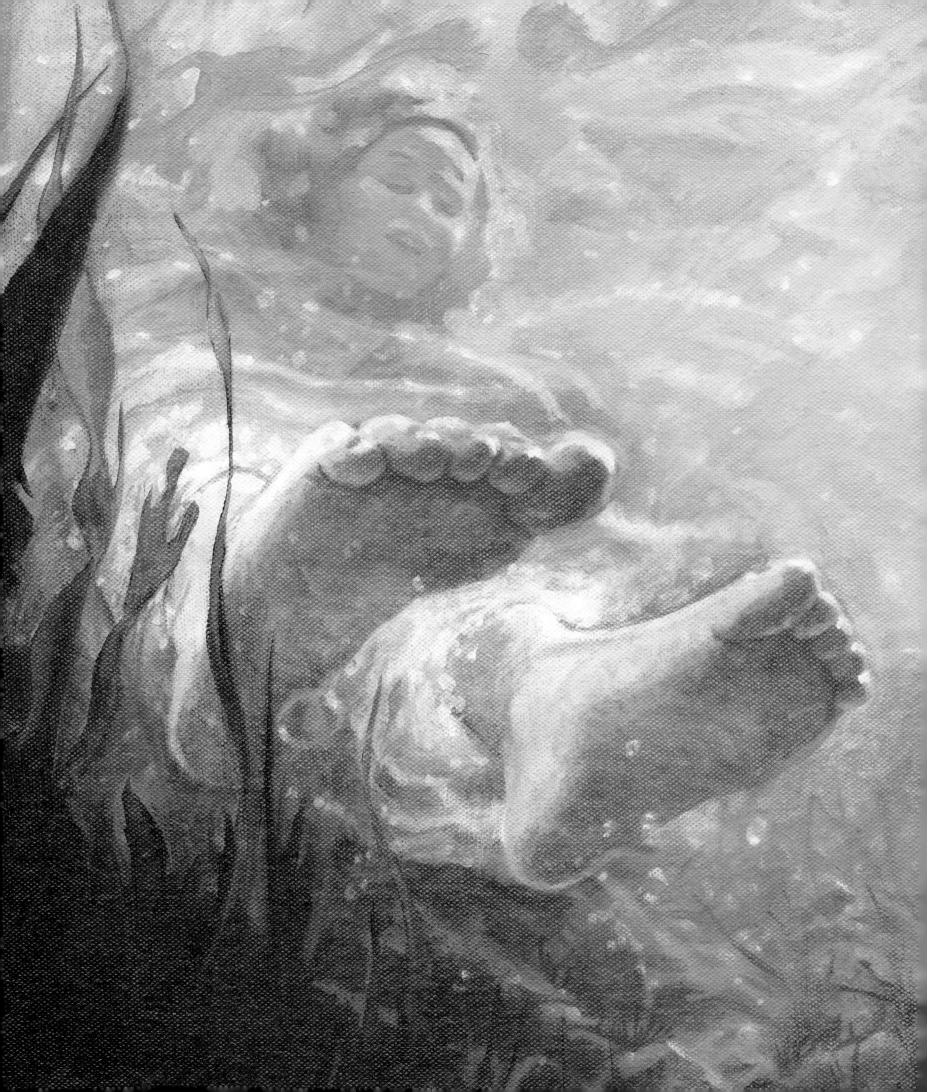

No one but you can see the morning sun sparkle
   on the water
   as you dangle your toes
   and watch a sunfish dart behind a stump
   and see the miraculous marching of a water strider across
      the surface of a pond.

No one but you can gently hold
　　a turtle with your own hands
　　and count the plates on her back
　　and the stripes on her chin,
　　feel the hardness of her shell
　　and the soft scratching of her claws,
　　and imagine what a turtle's life is like
　　as she swims back into the blue-green shadows
　　　　of her world.

Only one person can notice
    the hum of a bumblebee on a lazy afternoon
    as he buzzes past your ear
    on his way to a clover patch,
    and that someone is no one but you.

And who else but you will roll a glistening dewdrop
        from a rose petal onto your tongue
        or savor a red, ripe strawberry
        or a golden drop of honey
        and know what it tastes like
        just to you?

No one but you can smell the moist earth
    after a rain shower,
    discovering just the way it smells to you,
    or catch the fragrance of a tulip
    or an apple blossom
    or even a dandelion.

No one else can blow parachute seeds into the wind
   with your breath
   or whistle with a blade of grass
   held between your two thumbs
   or sing your very own song
   with your very own voice
   in your very own way.

No one but you can hold a puppy
    in your gentle arms,
    feel the softness of its muzzle
    and the warm tickle of its tongue,
    and make it feel safe and cared for
    just because it's with you.

No one but you can smile just your smile
    or laugh just your laugh.

No one but you can remember
    your own memories . . .
    all the things you've done,
    all the places you've been,
    with all your favorite people.
    And, of course, no one but you can
    make your new memories —
    the ones yet to come.

No one but you can hear chorus frogs
singing on a spring night
under a blanket of stars
just like you can.

No one else in the world can look up at the stars,
these stars, right now,
with your own eyes,
and feel your own special place on this earth.

And no one else can wish upon that star,
that *very* one,
from just where you stand
and wish your very own wish.
No one but you.

And no one — no one in all the wide world but you —
can feel the feelings in your heart,
knowing that someone loves you . . .

and saying the words only your lips can say:
"I love you, too."

No one but you.

To Kathy Ann, with love
D. W.

For Nicole, Nicholas, and Chitra
P. J. L.

With special thanks to Willow, Yasmin, Jason-Mogga,
Emma, Maya, Ben, Sam, Evie, Rosebelle, and Chitra

First edition 2011

Library of Congress Cataloging-in-Publication Data

Wood, Douglas, date.
No one but you / Douglas Wood. — 1st ed.
p. cm.
Summary: The reader is invited to discover nature using their sense of smell, sight,
hearing, touch, and taste.
ISBN 978-0-7636-3848-1
[1. Nature — Fiction. 2. Senses and sensation — Fiction.] I. Title.
PZ7.W84738No 2010
[E] — dc22   2008025503

11 12 13 14 15 16 SWT 10 9 8 7 6 5 4 3 2 1

Printed in Dongguan, Guangdong, China

This book was typeset in Golden Cockerel ITC.
The illustrations were done in oil.

Candlewick Press
99 Dover Street
Somerville, Massachusetts 02144

visit us at www.candlewick.com